MR. TAXI

Written by Mia Emery   Illustrated by María Fló

With a full and grateful heart, this book is dedicated
to my family and friends ... passed ... and present ...
forever connected by an invisible thread~

Visit invisiblethreadpublishing.com to explore the world of Mr. Taxi further
and click on the "Grown–Ups" page for free printable learning activities.

Book design by Travis D. Peterson.

ISBN (Hardcover): 979-8-9852364-0-8
ISBN (Softcover): 979-8-9852364-1-5
ISBN (Digital eBook): 979-8-9852364-2-2
ISBN (Kindle Edition): 979-8-9852364-3-9

Library of Congress Control Number: 2022904473

invisiblethreadpublishing.com

TAkE TiME TO eNjOY THE pARk!

When young children are read to, a foundation is laid. Foundations are meant to be built upon, one step at a time, not necessarily to be finished ... but rather dynamic, to be constantly changing and progressing.

The park scenes within the pages of this book were created with intention. When reading, take time to pause on these quiet scenes, as they build on the foundation of human kindness and connection, traits to be reminded of these days and always. Allow time to discover relationships and socialization within these scenes.

Every individual holds a unique and precious gift.
What gifts will your readers find?

"Howdy, Misther Taxthi! I've been therching hard for you! We're going to the pool today! You thould paint your taxthi **BLUE**!"

"You're RIGHT!"
said Mr. Taxi, as he
honked his horn ...

BEEP!
BEEP!

"I'll make sure that
you can find me!"

And they ZiPPED
off down the street!

"Hey there, Mr. Taxi! I've got to get downtown! I'm really in a great big rush! Won't you paint your taxi **BROWN**?"

"Hey there, Mr. Taxi! Was that you way up ahead? I've been searching for you everywhere! Can you paint your taxi **ReD**?"

"Sure!" said Mr. Taxi, as he honked his horn ...

BEEP! BEEP!

"I'll make sure that you can find me!"

And they ZIPPED off down the street!

"Hey there, Mr. Taxi! You were nowhere to be seen. I've got to meet some children. Might you paint your taxi GREEN?"

"Hey there, Mr. Taxi! You seem like a nice fellow. But it's really hard to find you. Could you paint your taxi YELLOW?"

"Hey there, Mr. Taxi," said the lady, with a wink. "It's so very hard to spot you! Will you paint your taxi **PINK**?"

"Sure!" said Mr. Taxi, as he honked his horn ...

BEEP!
BEEP!

"I'll make sure that you can find me!"

And they ZIPPED off down the street!

LIBRARY

TAXI
STAND

"Hey there, Mr. Taxi! These dogs just want to play! We couldn't find you anywhere! Please paint your taxi **GRAY**!"

"Hey there, Mr. Taxi!
We've had a busy day!
But your taxi is so hard
to find! It should
NOT be painted **GRAY**!"

"Hooray!" cried all the people, as they hopped in the back seat. "Now we KNOW that we will find you!"

And they ZIPPED off
down the street!